DO YOU KNOW

PIPPI

LONGSTOCKING?

BY ASTRID LINDGREN WITH PICTURES

BY INGRID NYMAN

Translated by
Elisabeth Kallick Dyssegaard

R&S
BOOKS

Stockholm   New York   London   Adelaide   Toronto

Rabén & Sjögren Bokförlag, Stockholm
www.raben.se

Originally published in Sweden by Rabén & Sjögren under the title *Känner du Pippi Långstrump?*
Library of Congress catalog card number: 99-70430
Printed in Denmark
First American edition 1999. Fifth printing 2004
ISBN 91-29-64661-8

Rabén & Sjögren Bokförlag is part of
P. A. Norstedt & Söner Publishing Group, established in 1823

Here are Tommy and Annika, two nice, well-mannered little children. They are playing croquet in their yard. It's okay.

"But I'd still like to have a friend," says Annika.

"So would I," says Tommy.

Next to Tommy and Annika's yard is another yard. In it is a house called Villa Villekulla. No one lives there. The house is empty.

"It's so silly that no one wants to move into that house," says Tommy.

"Yes," says Annika. "Someone should live there. Someone with children."

One beautiful day when Tommy and Annika peer over the fence surrounding Villa Villekulla, they see something very strange. A little girl is walking across the yard, carrying a big horse. Tommy and Annika can't believe their eyes, because a little girl can't lift a horse. But this girl can. Her name is Pippi Longstocking, and she is so incredibly strong that there is not a policeman in the whole world who is as strong as she is. She is also rich. She has a big bag full of gold coins. And now she has moved into Villa Villekulla.

She's going to live there all alone with her horse and her little monkey, who is called Mr. Nilsson. Pippi has no mom or dad, which is fine with her, because that means there's no one to tell her that she has to go to bed just when she's having the most fun. She always does exactly as she pleases.

"Do you want to have breakfast at my house?" Pippi asks Tommy and Annika.

"Yes, thank you," they say.

"Who's cooking?" asks Annika.

"I am," says Pippi.

Pippi does everything herself. Now she is making pancakes. When a pancake is done, she throws it way up in the air and over to Tommy and Annika, who are sitting on the firewood chest, stuffing themselves.

"Those were the best pancakes I've ever had," says Tommy.

Pippi has a broken egg in her hair. It landed there when she was beating the pancake batter. But Pippi doesn't care.

"They say that egg yolks are good for your hair," she says. "Just wait, my hair will grow like crazy."

Pippi also bakes cookies. She rolls out the dough on the kitchen floor.

"Because the counter just isn't big enough when you are baking at least five hundred cookies," says Pippi.

Mr. Nilsson, the little monkey, helps her. But the horse isn't allowed to help. He lives on the veranda (which is why you can't see him in the picture).

"Why on earth do you keep your horse on the veranda?" asks Tommy. All the horses he knows live in stables.

"Well," says Pippi, "in the kitchen he'd just be in the way. And he doesn't feel comfortable in the living room."

After a while, Tommy and Annika go home. But they are very happy to have a new friend.

Pippi can braid her hair and button her undershirt at the same time. Not many people can do that.

Here she is eating. She lies on the table and puts her food on the chair. There's nobody to tell her to sit properly.

When she washes herself, she dips her whole head in the washbasin. She likes to get water in her eyes.

Once in a while, she'll scrub the kitchen floor. She straps brushes on her feet and pours a whole bucket of water onto the floor. Then she skates on the brushes.

When she chops wood, she never splits
fewer than five pieces at a time.

Yuck, the stove is full of smoke. Pippi has to
go up on the roof and clean the chimney.
She does everything herself.

"I'm a thing-finder," says Pippi one day to Tommy and Annika.

"A thing-finder, what's that?" asks Tommy.

"A person who finds things," says Pippi. "The whole world is full of things, and someone needs to find them. And that's what a thing-finder does."

Tommy and Annika decide to become thing-finders as well. Then they all go out searching for things.

Pippi finds a rusty metal can.

"You can never have too many cans," she says with satisfaction.

"What can you use it for?" wonders Tommy.

"You can stick your head in it and pretend it's the middle of the night," says Pippi.

And she does. She walks along with the can over her head until she trips over a fence. What a racket! But Pippi finds something else. An empty spool.

"Such a sweet, sweet little spool to blow bubbles with or to hang around your neck on a string," she says happily.

Tommy and Annika haven't found anything.

"Why don't you look inside those tree stumps," says Pippi. Tree stumps are among the best places for thing-finders.

And guess what! Tommy finds a nice notebook with a little silver pen. And Annika finds a coral necklace.

Then the thing-finders go home – Pippi with her can and spool, Tommy with his notebook, and Annika with her necklace.

The circus is in town. Pippi buys
tickets for herself and Tommy
and Annika with one of
her many gold coins.
Pippi has never been
to the circus. She
doesn't know
how it works.

She wants to perform, too. Because Pippi can do anything. The circus director gets mad. The girl who was supposed to walk on the high wire gets mad, too. But the people at the circus shout, "Go, Pippi!"

A pretty little circus girl comes riding in on a horse. She can stand up on her horse. But so can Pippi. She jumps up on the horse's back and stands behind the circus girl. The circus girl tries to push her off. She doesn't know how strong Pippi is.

"Why should you be the only one having fun," says Pippi to the circus girl. "I've paid, too."

"Go, Pippi!" scream Tommy and Annika and all the people at the circus.

Pippi knows even more tricks. The strongest man in the world is next. Big Anton is his name. The circus director promises a reward to the person who can wrestle Big Anton to the floor.

"I can," says Pippi to Tommy and Annika.

"Even you can't do that," says Annika. "He's the strongest man in the
world."

"And I am the strongest girl," says
Pippi.

She goes right over to Big Anton
and grabs him around the waist. He's
so surprised that his eyes almost pop
out of his head when he sees that such
a little girl wants to wrestle with him.
But – one, two, three – Pippi throws
him up in the air and then she lays him
down on the floor.

"Pippi's won, Pippi's won!" scream
the people at the circus.

When Pippi sleeps, she always puts her feet on the pillow and her head under the covers. That's how she likes to sleep, and there's no one to tell her not to. Mr. Nilsson sleeps in a green doll's bed, but he doesn't put his feet on the pillow.

One dark night, two nasty robbers climb into Pippi's room. They want to steal the big bag with all the gold coins. They have no idea that Pippi is so strong.

"Ha, ha, we'll soon have the bag," they say. And they snatch it.

But then Pippi shoots up out of bed. In no time she's taken back the bag.

"We're not kidding," says one robber. "Give me that bag!" And he grabs Pippi's arm hard.

"I'm not kidding, either," says Pippi. She throws him up on top of a wardrobe. Then she throws the other robber up there, too.

Both robbers are so scared they start to cry. Pippi feels sorry for them and gives them each a gold coin to buy food. Because Pippi is nice. Someone who is very strong has to be very nice also.

Soon it will be Pippi's birthday. And, of course, she is going to have a birth-day party. She writes a letter to Tommy and Annika inviting them to the party. She doesn't write very well, because she hasn't gone to school like other children. But she does her best. Then she sneaks over and puts the letter in Tommy and Annika's mailbox.

Tommy and Annika are so happy when they find the letter. They can't wait to go to Pippi's party. They put on their nicest clothes and brush their hair. And, of course, they buy a present for Pippi. They buy a music box and wrap it. They both hold the package when they go to Villa Villekulla.

When Pippi opens her present, she's so excited that she jumps up and down. She plays the music box for a long time. It has a pretty tune.

Pippi has set the kitchen table. She serves Tommy and Annika hot chocolate with whipped cream and lots of cookies and cake. She baked everything herself. Mr. Nilsson is sitting on the table. Pippi's horse has also been invited to the party.

"I've never been to a birthday party with a horse before," says Annika, and gives the horse a lump of sugar.

"Me, neither," says Tommy. "This is the best party I've ever been to."

When Pippi has had her hot chocolate, she puts her cup upside down on her head like a hat. But it isn't completely empty. A little hot chocolate trickles down her face.

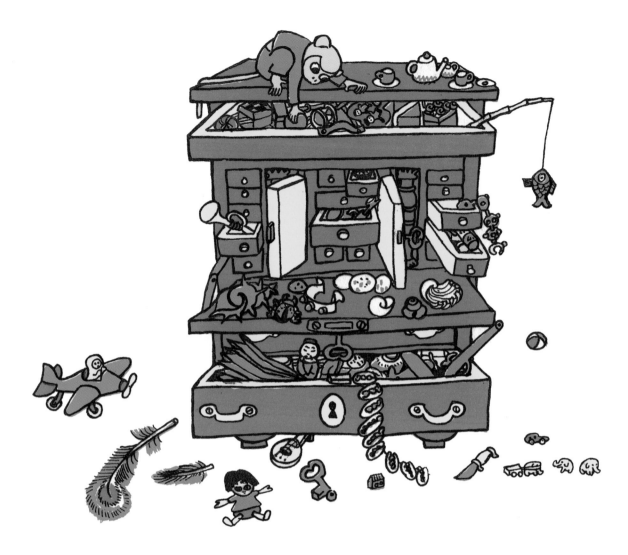

Afterward they play a game called Don't Touch the Floor. You play by climbing around the kitchen without ever touching the floor. They jump from the sink to the stove and from the stove to the firewood chest and then they crawl across the shelf to the table and then up onto the cupboard in the corner and from the cupboard to the horse and from the horse back to the sink. It's a good thing the horse is there, so they can climb on him, too.

Pippi has a desk with many tiny drawers. There are more magical things in that desk than in a whole toy store. There are small dolls' dishes and trumpets, birds' eggs and unusual snail shells, knives with mother-of-pearl handles, and necklaces. In fact, there's too much to list it all. Pippi wants to give Tommy and Annika a present, even though it's not their birthday. Tommy gets a little ivory flute. Annika gets a brooch that looks like a butterfly.

"That was the best party I've ever been to," says Tommy.

"Yes, if only we could stay forever," says Annika.

They wave to Pippi, and Pippi and Mr. Nilsson wave back.

Tommy and Annika have such a good time with Pippi they want to play with her every day.